© 1989 Verlag Heinrich Ellermann München

© English translation Century Hutchinson Ltd 1989

All rights reserved
First published in 1989 by Ellermann Verlag
First published in Great Britain in 1989 by Hutchinson Children's Books
An imprint of Century Hutchinson Ltd
Brookmount House, 62-65 Chandos Place,
Covent Garden, London WC2N 4NW

Century Hutchinson Australia (Pty) Ltd
88-91 Albion Street, Surry Hills, NSW 2010

Century Hutchinson New Zealand Limited
32-34 View Road, PO Box 40-086, Glenfield, Auckland 10

Century Hutchinson South Africa (Pty) Ltd
PO Box 337, Bergvlei 2012, South Africa

Printed and bound in Germany

Set in Goudy Old Style

ISBN 0 09 174141 6

Elisabeth Reuter

Christopher's Story

Translated by Patricia Crampton

HUTCHINSON

London   Sydney   Auckland   Johannesburg

It was Christopher's birthday. His best friends, Daniel and Jason, were coming to tea. Christopher should have been looking forward to his birthday party but he was tired and he even had a slight temperature. Christopher was not enjoying life as much as he used to.

'I want to see you dashing about like a wild boy again,' said his mother, 'but you bruise so easily now. I think we should go and see the doctor.'

At first, the doctor thought Christopher's clown, Maxie, was the patient. He took a blood test from Maxie and Christopher had to comfort the clown and explain to the doctor that *he* was the one who got bruises and felt tired all the time. Maxie was always well and did not bruise at all!

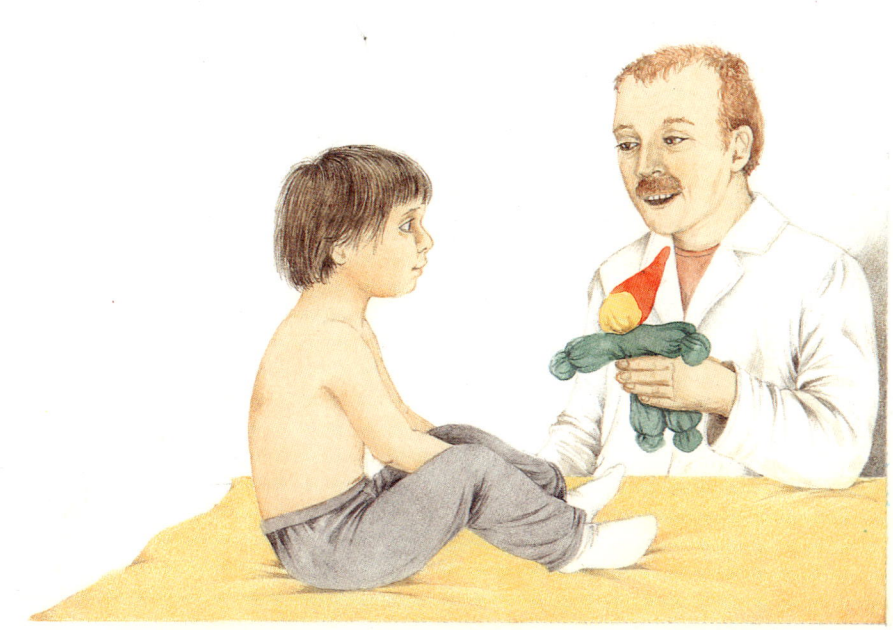

A few days later the doctor had a long talk with Christopher's mum and dad, and then they had a talk with Christopher. 'It's your blood that is not very well,' said his mother. 'That's why you get bruises and run a temperature. But now that we know what's wrong it has to be made better in hospital, where they have all the right things. The doctor would like you to go there tomorrow.'

'But I don't want to go to hospital,' Christopher whispered. 'I want to get better at home.'

'Hospitals are not bad places,' said his father, 'and Mummy or I will come to see you every day. Not that you will be lonely! There will be lots of other boys and girls there too.'

'Can Maxie come?' said Christopher.

'Of course he can,' said Mum. 'Put together anything you want to take.'

His sister Ruth helped him to pack his own small case for the hospital and told Christopher about the time she had been there to have her tonsils out and had had almost nothing but ice cream to eat. 'I got really sick of it!' she said.

As soon as Christopher had been tucked into his hospital bed, his mother read him a story. When she had gone, a friendly lady doctor came to explain about the tests she was going to do to find out all about the sick cells in Christopher's blood.

Then a thin needle was bandaged to Christopher's hand. The thin needle was joined on to a long, thin pipe, and the pipe was joined on to a fat bottle, from which drops of medicine flowed down into Christopher's hand, to fight the sick cells.

Christopher was amazed when he saw Simon, the boy in the next bed. Simon was completely bald! He had the same sickness as Christopher, and he knew a great deal about it. It was called leukaemia and, during the treatment, his hair had fallen out, but it would grow again when the treatment was finished. 'I'm Simon Egghead now,' he said with a grin, 'but I've got a coloured cap to wear if my head gets cold, just like the one I wear when it's snowing.'

The next day, Christopher asked his mother to knit him a woolly hat like Simon's. It was lucky Maxie already had a woolly cap, because he had never had any hair at all!

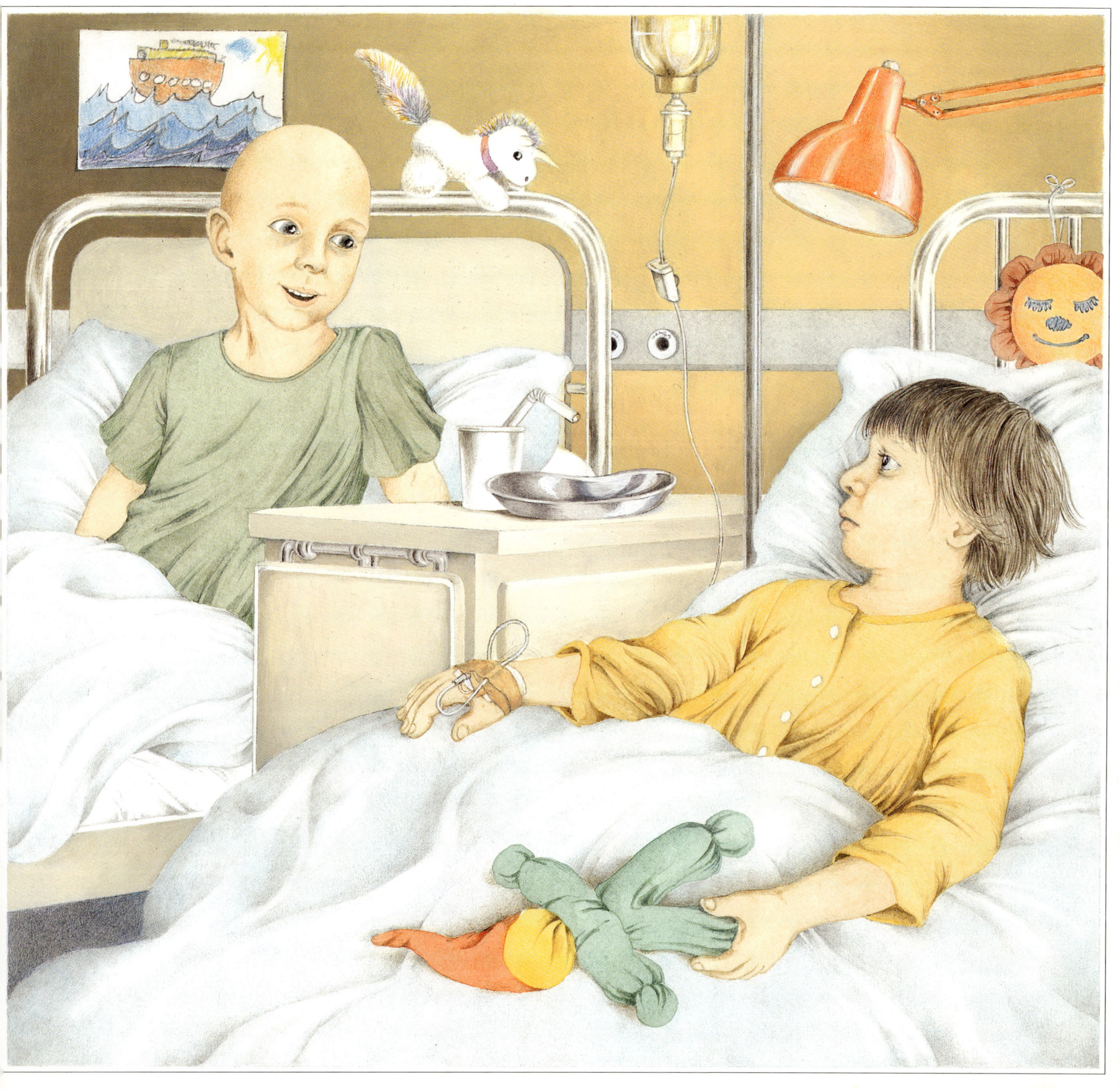

Whenever Christopher felt well enough, he could go to the playroom with some of the other children. He especially liked a girl called Sarah, who walked about with her bottle stand and a drip in the back of her hand just like his.

The book trolley came around once a week and he was allowed to borrow as many books as he liked, but his favourite was the puppet theatre that sometimes performed in the big hall.

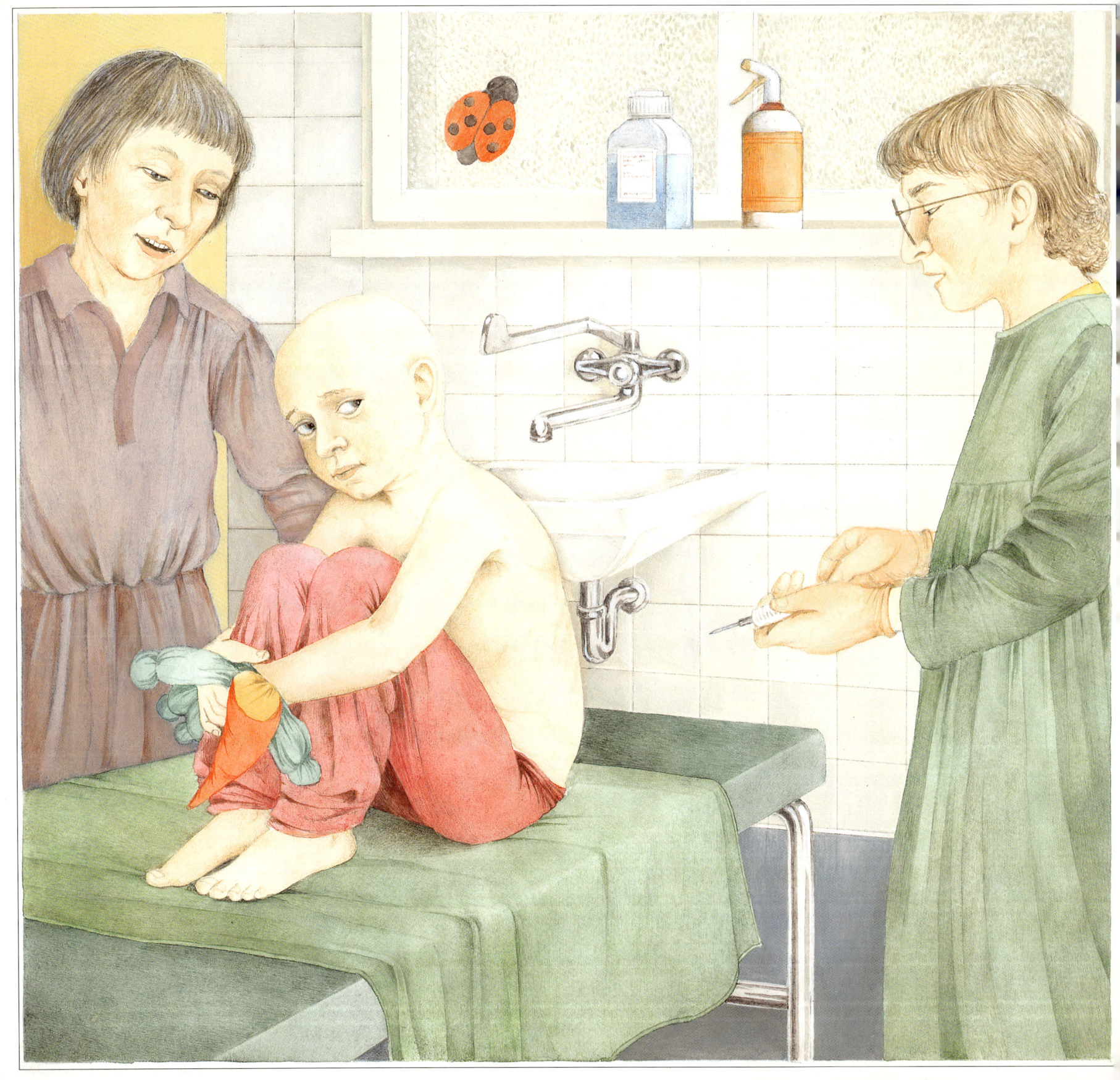

There were also some difficult days, when the nurses and doctors seemed too busy to stop and talk to Christopher. And some of the medicines made him feel awful. 'Funny sort of medicine,' he said to Simon. 'It makes me feel worse, not better!'

For a test called a 'lumbar puncture' he had to curl up small and not move a muscle. 'I didn't know punctures could hurt,' said Christopher. 'I'll remember, next time the car gets one.' But the doctor had explained to him that this was the only way to find out if there were any of the sick cells left in his blood, so he tried not to mind too much.

He was feeling a little better every day, too, and at last the doctor said he could go home on Saturday. 'We'll give you some pills to take,' she said, 'and we want to see you again now and then, to make sure you are keeping well.'

Christopher said goodbye to Simon and the other children and went happily down to the hall with his case to wait for his parents.

A few days later Ruth and Christopher went to the big playground again and Christopher was pleased to see Jason and Daniel building a huge castle in the sand pit. But when he ran over to them, his friends did not even look up. 'Can I help?' said Christopher.

'My parents said I mustn't play with you,' said Jason. 'You've got a funny illness, and we might catch it.'

'Leukaemia isn't catching!' Christopher shouted. 'And anyway, I haven't got it any more and I'm coming back to school, too!'

'I don't know,' said Jason. 'I'd better go home.' And off he ran, with Daniel close behind him.

Ruth and Christopher went home, too. Christopher wanted to see his mother. 'There are lots of people who are frightened of illness, I'm afraid,' she said, hugging him. 'But it's really because they don't know anything about it. We'll ask Jason and Daniel and their parents to come over, and we'll explain it all to them so that they won't be afraid.' After that Jason and Daniel played with Christopher as much as he liked, and Christopher felt quite strange and grown up all of a sudden; he knew much more about a rare disease than his friends' parents did!

Ruth was not so happy, though. She always had to be thinking of her little brother; keeping quiet while he had his afternoon rest, and doing some of the household jobs that Christopher would usually have done, so that he didn't get too tired.

One day she lost her temper. 'You love Christopher more than me!' she yelled at her mother. 'I wish I had leukaemia too, then you'd do things with me like you used to!'

'Of course we love you both the same,' said her mother, giving Ruth a big hug. 'We've been so worried about Chris that we forgot to worry about you. We're just happy that you're well. I'm so sorry, Ruthie! Let's make a plan this minute.'

Ruth and her mother decided to write a list of things that Ruth could do with her mum or dad on their own. Of course, Christopher wanted to make a list, too. So in the end they made a big coloured chart of the things they all wanted to do.

Christopher's hair was growing again and he was back at school, but most of all he was looking forward to the summer holidays, when they were all going to stay on a farm. But the day before they were going he began to cough again, his temperature went up and he felt very tired.

'Hospital first,' said his mother. 'We can always go on holiday later.'

That was not at all what Christopher wanted, but when his parents rang the hospital, the doctor said she would like him to come in right away. Ruth was just as disappointed, but Dad found some things on her list that they could do together, while Mum drove Christopher to the hospital.

The leukaemia cells were back in Christopher's blood. He was so furious that he went under the bedclothes with Maxie and refused to talk to anyone.

Christopher's doctor came in. 'This is when we start fighting,' she told him. 'I'm not a bit pleased about the leukaemia coming back, either, and it doesn't happen often. But now that it has, we have to do all the things that made you well before – the drip and injections and that strong medicine.'

'I don't want any more drip, I don't want any injections!' cried Christopher, kicking off the covers and waving his arms wildly. 'I want to have a different illness!'

When he had quietened down, the doctor stroked his arm gently. 'The best thing you can do is to give the leukaemia a good kick!' she said. 'I'm glad to see how strong you are. We're going to fight the leukaemia together, and use all your anger to see it off!'

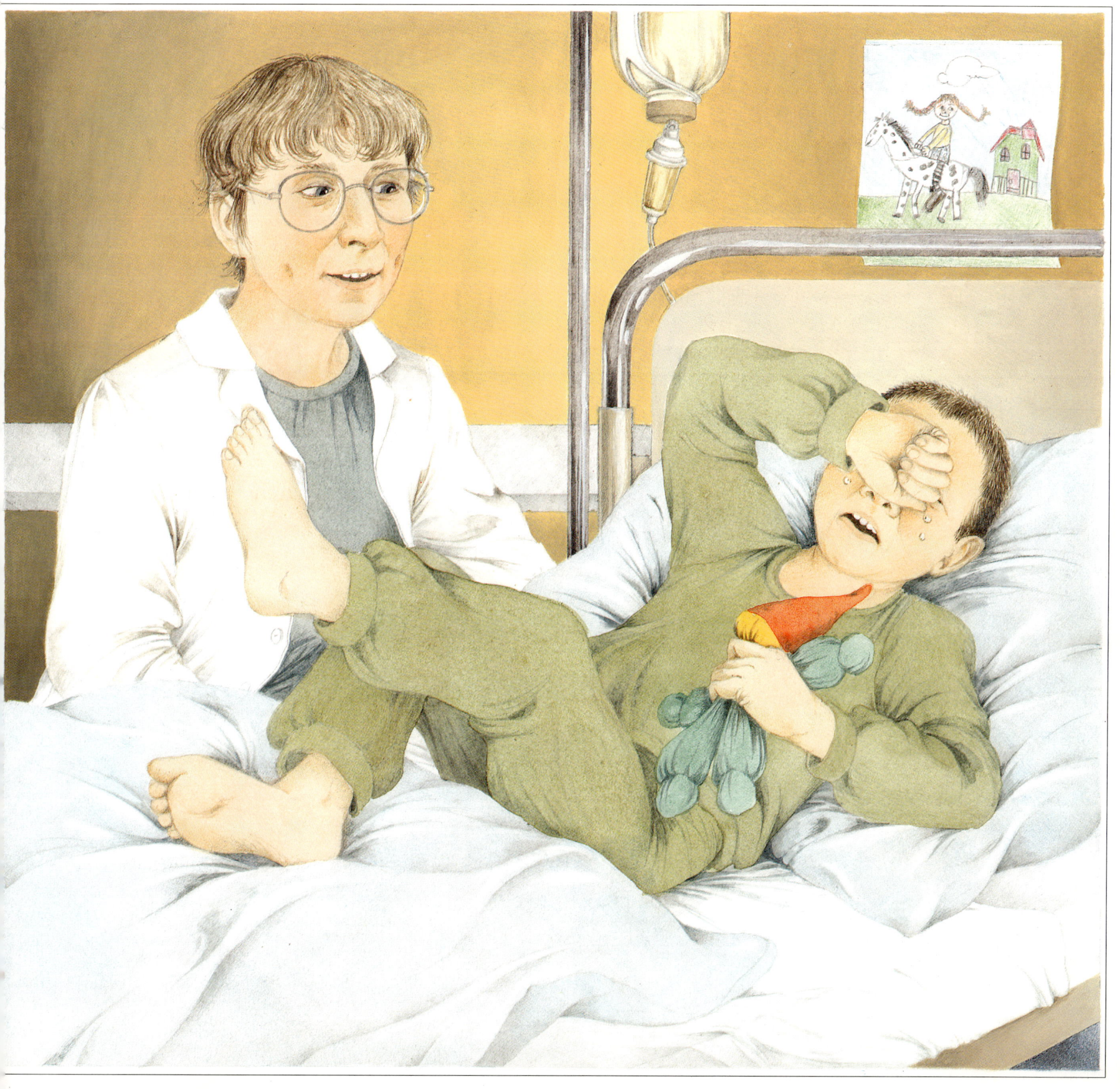

This time Christopher knew exactly what was happening, and when he had the 'drip' in his hand again he pretended that the tiny drops were hundreds of tiny Christophers marching into his blood to fight the bad cells and make him strong. And he worked out a special way of breathing so that the injections did not hurt too much – besides, he had a game with the nurse that, if they really pricked, he could pinch her! Maxie was not at all sad, either, because he really liked seeing the other toys in the playroom. There was even another clown! Christopher enjoyed playing with the other children, too, though his friends Simon and Sarah had gone home. Now he had a new friend, whose name was Mandy.

'Perhaps there are worse illnesses than ours,' said Mandy. 'What if you couldn't see! I'm glad I can see you.'

Christopher laughed and put his arms round her. 'Me too,' he said. But as Christopher grew stronger, Mandy was growing weaker. She had her own room now, so that her parents could take it in turns to sleep in the other bed. Christopher waved to her whenever the door was open.

One morning Dad arrived to find Christopher hiding under the bedclothes again. 'What's the matter, Chris?' Dad asked, anxiously. He lifted Christopher on to his lap, and after a time Christopher told him.

'Mandy died last night,' he whispered. 'She had leukaemia too. Am I going to die?'

'We all have to die one day,' said Dad, 'but for Mandy it happened while she was still young. No one really understands about death, but I believe part of Mandy stays with us, even though we can't see her.'

'Look, Dad, I've got a picture of her. Her mother gave it to me to look at when I'm thinking about her.' Christopher and his father looked at Mandy's photograph together. 'I would like to have gone on playing with her,' said Christopher, 'but she was awfully tired.'

'And you're getting stronger all the time,' said Dad.

Soon afterwards, the doctor telephoned Christopher's parents. 'Christopher can go home now,' she told them. 'No sign of leukaemia at all!' They came to pick him up at once and drove home with Christopher between them.

'Do you know why the leukaemia has gone away?' he asked his parents. They shook their heads. 'It's because I fought it so hard that it's sick and tired of me, and it's gone home to have a rest!'

His father laughed. 'And now we're all going to have a rest, too,' he said. 'We're going to the farm for the REST of the holidays.' Christopher and his mother groaned and laughed at the same time.

Ruth was waiting excitedly at home, and Jason and Daniel were there too, with a big chocolate cake for Christopher. He looked round at them all without speaking. Somehow all the things he had been through, some painful, some sad, some happy and funny, had come together and become a part of him – and they had made him strong.